**Put Beginning Readers on the Right Track with
ALL ABOARD READING™**

The All Aboard Reading series is especially designed for beginning readers. Written by noted authors and illustrated in full color, these are books that children really want to read—books to excite their imagination, expand their interests, make them laugh, and support their feelings. With fiction and nonfiction stories that are high interest and curriculum-related, All Aboard Reading books offer something for every young reader. And with four different reading levels, the All Aboard Reading series lets you choose which books are most appropriate for your children and their growing abilities.

Picture Readers
Picture Readers have super-simple texts, with many nouns appearing as rebus pictures. At the end of each book are 24 flash cards—on one side is a rebus picture; on the other side is the written-out word.

Station Stop 1
Station Stop 1 books are best for children who have just begun to read. Simple words and big type make these early reading experiences more comfortable. Picture clues help children to figure out the words on the page. Lots of repetition throughout the text helps children to predict the next word or phrase—an essential step in developing word recognition.

Station Stop 2
Station Stop 2 books are written specifically for children who are reading with help. Short sentences make it easier for early readers to understand what they are reading. Simple plots and simple dialogue help children with reading comprehension.

Station Stop 3
Station Stop 3 books are perfect for children who are reading alone. With longer text and harder words, these books appeal to children who have mastered basic reading skills. More complex stories captivate children who are ready for more challenging books.

In addition to All Aboard Reading books, look for All Aboard Math Readers™ (fiction stories that teach math concepts children are learning in school); All Aboard Science Readers™ (nonfiction books that explore the most fascinating science topics in age-appropriate language); All Aboard Poetry Readers™ (funny, rhyming poems for readers of all levels); and All Aboard Mystery Readers™ (puzzling tales where children piece together evidence with the characters).

All Aboard for happy reading!

American Greetings with rose logo is a trademark of AGC, Inc.

GROSSET & DUNLAP
Published by the Penguin Group
Penguin Group (USA) Inc., 375 Hudson Street, New York, New York 10014, U.S.A.
Penguin Group (Canada), 90 Eglinton Avenue East, Suite 700, Toronto,
Ontario, Canada M4P 2Y3
(a division of Pearson Penguin Canada Inc.)
Penguin Books Ltd, 80 Strand, London WC2R 0RL, England
Penguin Ireland, 25 St Stephen's Green, Dublin 2, Ireland
(a division of Penguin Books Ltd)
Penguin Group (Australia), 250 Camberwell Road, Camberwell, Victoria 3124, Australia
(a division of Pearson Australia Group Pty Ltd)
Penguin Books India Pvt Ltd, 11 Community Centre, Panchsheel Park,
New Delhi - 110 017, India
Penguin Group (NZ), 67 Apollo Drive, Mairangi Bay, Auckland 1311, New Zealand
(a division of Pearson New Zealand Ltd.)
Penguin Books (South Africa) (Pty) Ltd, 24 Sturdee Avenue, Rosebank,
Johannesburg 2196, South Africa
Penguin Books Ltd, Registered Offices:
80 Strand, London WC2R 0RL, England

The publisher does not have any control over and does not assume any responsibility for author or third-party websites or their content.

Library of Congress Cataloging-in-Publication Data

Bryant, Megan E.
Dance with me! / by Megan E. Bryant ; illustrated by MJ Illustrations.
p. cm. — (All aboard reading. Station stop 1)
"Strawberry Shortcake."
Summary: When Strawberry Shortcake and her friend Ginger both want to do the ballet solo in the dance show, they decide to do a duet instead so they do not have to compete against each other.
ISBN 978-0-448-44665-3 (pbk.)
[1. Dance—Fiction. 2. Cooperativeness—Fiction.] I. MJ Illustrations (Group) II. Title.
PZ7.B83945Dan 2007
[E]—dc22
2007002971
10 9 8 7 6 5 4 3 2 1

Dance with Me!

By Megan E. Bryant

Illustrated by MJ Illustrations

Grosset & Dunlap

Strawberry Shortcake
loves to dance.

Her friends love to dance, too!

Strawberry has a berry
good idea.
The girls can put on a
dance show!

Each girl will have
a <u>solo</u>.
That means she will
dance all by herself.

Blueberry Muffin wants to
do the tap-dance solo.

Angel Cake wants to do
the jazz-dance solo.

Orange Blossom wants to
do the hip-hop solo.

Strawberry Shortcake wants to do the ballet solo.

But Ginger Snap wants to
do the ballet solo, too!
Which girl will get it?

Each girl will have to
try out.
The best dancer will
get the solo.

Strawberry goes home.
She practices all by
herself.

Ginger goes home.

She practices all by herself.

Dancing alone is not
berry friendly.

Dancing alone is not berry fun.

It is time to try out for the solo.

Strawberry is a little scared.

Ginger is a little scared, too.

Then Strawberry has a
berry good idea.
She and Ginger can share
the solo!

The girls will do a
ballet <u>duet</u>.
They will dance
together!

The girls practice and practice.
At last, it is time
for the dance show!

Blueberry starts the show
with a tap-dance solo.

Then Angel does a jazz-dance solo.

Next Orange does a
hip-hop solo.

At last, Strawberry and Ginger go onstage. They dance the berry best ballet duet—together!

Berry good job!

Take a bow, girls!